Sky Pony Press books may be purchased in bulk at special discounts for sales promotion, corporate gifts, fund-raising, or educational purposes. Special editions can also be created to specifications. For details, contact the Special Sales Department, Sky Pony Press, 307 West 36th Street, 11th Floor, New York, NY 10018 or info@skyhorsepublishing.com.

Sky Pony® is a registered trademark of Skyhorse Publishing, Inc.®, a Delaware corporation.

Visit our website at www.skyponypress.com
Books, authors, and more at www.skyponypressblog.com

www.kaylaharren.com

10 9 8 7 6 5 4 3 2 1

Library of Congress Cataloging-in-Publication Data available on file.

Manufactured in China, April 2017
This product conforms to CPSIA 2008

Cover illustration by Kayla Harren
Cover design by Sammy Yuen

Hardcover ISBN: 978-1-5107-1635-3
Ebook ISBN: 978-1-5107-1636-0

MARY HAD A LITTLE LIZARD

Kayla Harren

Today Is Painting Day!
painting words:
paint water paper towels
easel brushes

blue
yellow
red

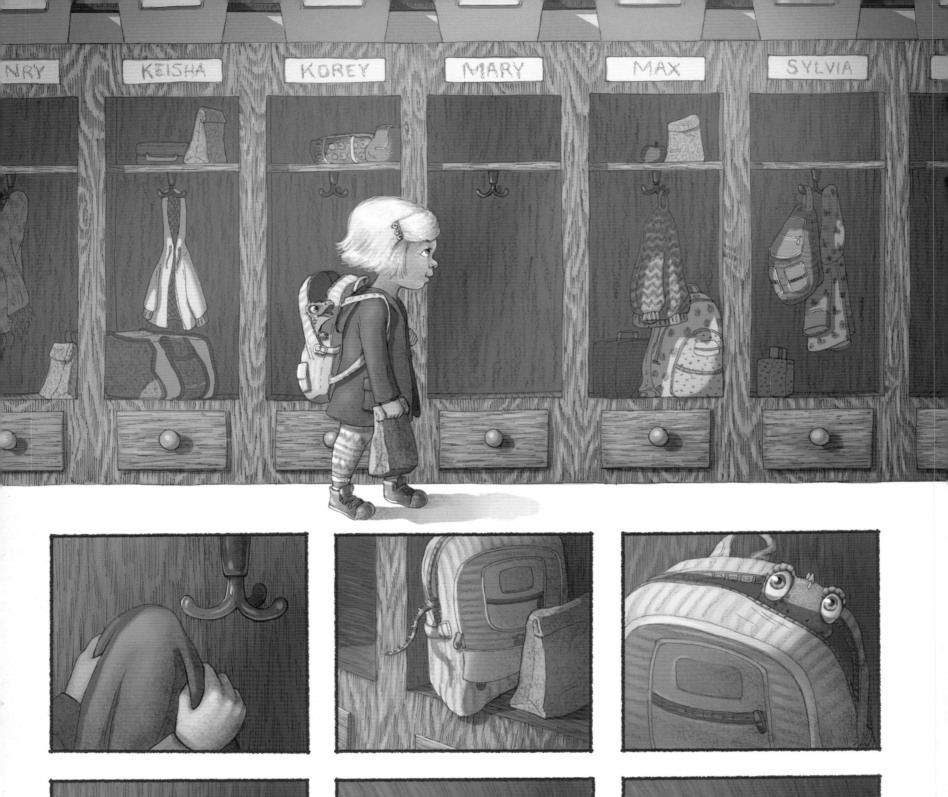

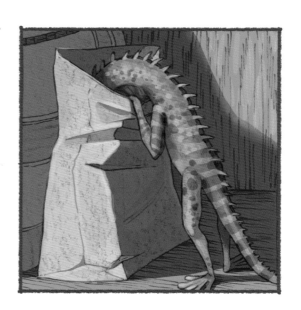